The Tortoise and the Hare

Retold by Michèle Dufresne • Illustrated by Ann Caranci

PIONEER VALLEY EDUCATIONAL PRESS, INC.

"I am fast," said the hare.
"Who will race with me?"

"I will race with you," said the tortoise. "We can race to the big tree."

4

"Ha! Ha! Ha!"
said the hare.
"**You** can't beat me!"

"We will see,"
said the tortoise.

6

Off went the hare.
Off went the tortoise.

9

The hare ran fast.
He ran and ran
down the road.
"I am so fast," said the hare.
"I will take a little nap."
He sat down
and went to sleep.

The tortoise did not stop.
He walked and walked.
He walked and walked
and walked.

The hare woke up.
He saw the tortoise
at the big tree.

"Oh, no!" said the hare. "I lost the race."

Slow but steady wins the race.